DREAMWORKS®
SHREK FOREVER AFTER™
MAD LIBS®

By Roger Price and Leonard Stern

PSS!
PRICE STERN SLOAN

An Imprint of Penguin Group (USA) Inc.

PRICE STERN SLOAN
Published by the Penguin Group
Penguin Group (USA) Inc., 375 Hudson Street, New York, New York 10014, USA
Penguin Group (Canada), 90 Eglinton Avenue East, Suite 700,
Toronto, Ontario M4P 2Y3, Canada
(a division of Pearson Penguin Canada Inc.)
Penguin Books Ltd., 80 Strand, London WC2R 0RL, England
Penguin Group Ireland, 25 St. Stephen's Green, Dublin 2, Ireland
(a division of Penguin Books Ltd.)
Penguin Group (Australia), 250 Camberwell Road, Camberwell, Victoria 3124, Australia
(a division of Pearson Australia Group Pty. Ltd.)
Penguin Books India Pvt. Ltd., 11 Community Centre,
Panchsheel Park, New Delhi—110 017, India
Penguin Group (NZ), 67 Apollo Drive, Rosedale, North Shore 0632, New Zealand
(a division of Pearson New Zealand Ltd.)
Penguin Books (South Africa) (Pty.) Ltd., 24 Sturdee Avenue,
Rosebank, Johannesburg 2196, South Africa

Penguin Books Ltd., Registered Offices: 80 Strand, London WC2R 0RL, England

Published by Price Stern Sloan,
a division of Penguin Young Readers Group,
345 Hudson Street, New York, New York 10014.

ISBN 978-0-8431-9963-5

1 3 5 7 9 10 8 6 4 2

MAD LIBS®

INSTRUCTIONS

MAD LIBS® is a game for people who don't like games!
It can be played by one, two, three, four, or forty.

• RIDICULOUSLY SIMPLE DIRECTIONS

In this tablet you will find stories containing blank spaces where words are
left out. One player, the **READER**, selects one of these stories. The **READER**
does not tell anyone what the story is about. Instead, he/she asks the other
players, the **WRITERS**, to give him/her words. These words are used to fill
in the blank spaces in the story.

• TO PLAY

The **READER** asks each **WRITER** in turn to call out words—an adjective or
a noun or whatever the space calls for—and uses them to fill in the blank
spaces in the story. The result is a **MAD LIBS®** game.

When the **READER** then reads the completed **MAD LIBS®** game to the
other players, they will discover that they have written a story that is
fantastic, screamingly funny, shocking, silly, crazy, or just plain dumb—
depending upon which words each **WRITER** called out.

• EXAMPLE (Before and After)

"_____!" he said _____
     EXCLAMATION   ADVERB

as he jumped into his convertible _____ and
            NOUN

drove off with his _____ wife.
       ADJECTIVE

"_____*Ouch*_____!" he said _____*stupidly*_____
     EXCLAMATION   ADVERB

as he jumped into his convertible _____*cat*_____ and
            NOUN

drove off with his _____*brave*_____ wife.
       ADJECTIVE

MAD LIBS®

QUICK REVIEW

In case you have forgotten what adjectives, adverbs, nouns, and verbs are, here is a quick review:

An **ADJECTIVE** describes something or somebody. *Lumpy, soft, ugly, messy,* and *short* are adjectives.

An **ADVERB** tells how something is done. It modifies a verb and usually ends in "ly." *Modestly, stupidly, greedily,* and *carefully* are adverbs.

A **NOUN** is the name of a person, place, or thing. *Sidewalk, umbrella, bridle, bathtub,* and *nose* are nouns.

A **VERB** is an action word. *Run, pitch, jump,* and *swim* are verbs. Put the verbs in past tense if the directions say PAST TENSE. *Ran, pitched, jumped,* and *swam* are verbs in the past tense.

When we ask for **A PLACE**, we mean any sort of place: a country or city *(Spain, Cleveland)* or a room *(bathroom, kitchen).*

An **EXCLAMATION** or **SILLY WORD** is any sort of funny sound, gasp, grunt, or outcry, like *Wow!, Ouch!, Whomp!, Ick!,* and *Gadzooks!*

When we ask for specific words, like a **NUMBER**, a **COLOR**, an **ANIMAL**, or a **PART OF THE BODY**, we mean a word that is one of those things, like *seven, blue, horse,* or *head.*

When we ask for a **PLURAL**, it means more than one. For example, *cat* pluralized is *cats.*

MAD LIBS® is fun to play with friends, but you can also play it by yourself! To begin with, DO NOT look at the story on the page below. Fill in the blanks on this page with the words called for. Then, using the words you have selected, fill in the blank spaces in the story.

Now you've created your own hilarious MAD LIBS® game!

BIG (GREEN) DADDY

VERB ENDING IN "ING" _reading_

PERSON IN ROOM _MOM_

ADJECTIVE _big_

ADJECTIVE _smelly_

PLURAL NOUN _farts_

VERB _burp_

NOUN _Far, Far Away_

PART OF THE BODY _ear_

NOUN _Puss in Boots_

ADJECTIVE _snuffly_

PART OF THE BODY _nose_

ADJECTIVE _soft_

ANIMAL _donkey_

NUMBER _1_

ADJECTIVE _greenish_

ADJECTIVE _bad_

MAD LIBS®
BIG (GREEN) DADDY

Hi, Shrek—I'm off to do some grocery _____

VERB ENDING IN "ING"

at the Swamp & Shop. If you could look after Fergus, Farkle, and

_____ while I'm gone, that would be_____!

PERSON IN ROOM   ADJECTIVE

Here are some _____ reminders for the day:

ADJECTIVE

• Donkey and his five little dronkey _____ are coming

PLURAL NOUN

over later to _____ with our kids. Please make sure they

VERB

don't burn down our _____!

NOUN

• Fergus shouldn't draw on Farkle's _____ with his

PART OF THE BODY

earwax crayons. And make sure Farkle doesn't hide Felicia's

favorite squeaky _____ .

NOUN

• If something smells so _____ it makes your

ADJECTIVE

_____ curl, it probably means a/an _____

PART OF THE BODY   ADJECTIVE

diaper needs to be changed.

• Give the kids a gourd bottle of _____ juice each before

ANIMAL

nap time and make sure they let out _____ burps. Better

NUMBER

out than _____, I always say!

ADJECTIVE

Love, Your _____ Fiona

ADJECTIVE

MAD LIBS® is fun to play with friends, but you can also play it by yourself! To begin with, DO NOT look at the story on the page below. Fill in the blanks on this page with the words called for. Then, using the words you have selected, fill in the blank spaces in the story.

Now you've created your own hilarious MAD LIBS® game!

YOU'RE INVITED

NUMBER _____

NOUN _____

ADJECTIVE _____

PLURAL NOUN _____

PLURAL NOUN _____

PLURAL NOUN _____

NOUN _____

ADJECTIVE _____

NOUN _____

NOUN _____

PLURAL NOUN _____

PART OF THE BODY _____

ADJECTIVE _____

PART OF THE BODY _____

ADJECTIVE _____

PERSON IN ROOM _____

ADJECTIVE _____

MAD LIBS®
YOU'RE INVITED

Fergus, Farkle, and Felicia are turning _____ years old—
NUMBER

and it's party time! Join us at The Candy _____ Family
NOUN

Fun Center for a/an _____ birthday celebration in their
ADJECTIVE

honor. It's being catered by the Three Little _____ Party
PLURAL NOUN

Planners, Inc. The menu includes enormous bowls of mud-covered

_____ and delicious, slug-encrusted _____.
PLURAL NOUN   PLURAL NOUN

And, of course, a chocolate birthday _____ to eat! Upon
NOUN

arrival, every _____ guest will be given a cone-shaped
ADJECTIVE

birthday _____ to wear. Everyone will get a chance to
NOUN

whack a/an _____-shaped piñata filled with yummy
NOUN

_____. And it wouldn't be a party without playing
PLURAL NOUN

Pin the _____ on Donkey. He doesn't mind. He's such
PART OF THE BODY

a/an _____ sport! There will also be _____
ADJECTIVE   PART OF THE BODY

painting, courtesy of the _____ Stepsisters, Doris and
ADJECTIVE

_____! A/an _____ time will be had by all!
PERSON IN ROOM   ADJECTIVE

MAD LIBS® is fun to play with friends, but you can also play it by yourself! To begin with, DO NOT look at the story on the page below. Fill in the blanks on this page with the words called for. Then, using the words you have selected, fill in the blank spaces in the story.

Now you've created your own hilarious MAD LIBS® game!

OGRE FOR A DAY

PERSON IN ROOM _____

ADJECTIVE _____

NUMBER _____

NOUN _____

ADJECTIVE _____

PLURAL NOUN _____

A PLACE _____

PLURAL NOUN _____

ADVERB _____

VERB ENDING IN "ING" _____

ADJECTIVE _____

TYPE OF LIQUID _____

NOUN _____

EXCLAMATION _____

ADJECTIVE _____

A PLACE _____

NOUN _____

ADJECTIVE _____

MAD LIBS®
OGRE FOR A DAY

I, _____, do hereby grant Rumpelstiltskin one
    PERSON IN ROOM

_____ day from my past in exchange for one _____-
ADJECTIVE   NUMBER

hour period during which I will once again feel like a real

_____. This agreement will guarantee, but not be limited to,
NOUN

the following _____ situations and events: I will be feared
                ADJECTIVE

and hated by all the _____ living in (the) _____.
                PLURAL NOUN   A PLACE

Villagers will chase me with pitchforks and flaming _____.
                                      PLURAL NOUN

But, when I roar _____, they will run, screaming and
                ADVERB

_____ in terror. I will be permitted to retreat to the
VERB ENDING IN "ING"

peace of my swamp where I will relax in a/an _____ mud
                                  ADJECTIVE

bath with a mug of frothy _____. I will feast on as many
                        TYPE OF LIQUID

roasted _____ rats as I want, and I won't be interrupted by
        NOUN

cries of "Da-Da!" or "_____!" Finally, I will have no obligation
            EXCLAMATION

to change _____ diapers or clean up (the) _____.
        ADJECTIVE   A PLACE

Disclaimer: Only true love's _____ will render this
                             NOUN

contract null and _____.
           ADJECTIVE

FROM SHREK FOREVER AFTER MAD LIBS® • Shrek Forever After ™ and © 2010 DreamWorks Animation L.L.C.
Shrek is a registered trademark of DreamWorks Animation L.L.C. All Rights Reserved.
Published by Price Stern Sloan, a division of Penguin Group (USA) Inc., 345 Hudson Street, New York, NY 10014.

MAD LIBS® is fun to play with friends, but you can also play it by yourself! To begin with, DO NOT look at the story on the page below. Fill in the blanks on this page with the words called for. Then, using the words you have selected, fill in the blank spaces in the story.

Now you've created your own hilarious MAD LIBS® game!

IT'S GOOD TO BE KING

ADJECTIVE _____

NOUN _____

PLURAL NOUN _____

A PLACE _____

NOUN _____

NOUN _____

PLURAL NOUN _____

PLURAL NOUN _____

PLURAL NOUN _____

NOUN _____

CELEBRITY _____

PERSON IN ROOM _____

ADJECTIVE _____

PART OF THE BODY (PLURAL) _____

ADJECTIVE _____

ADVERB _____

NOUN _____

PLURAL NOUN _____

MAD LIBS

IT'S GOOD TO BE KING

The life of a king is royally _____! At the Crone's
                                  ADJECTIVE

Nest Carriage Park, Rumpelstiltskin lived in a run-down, old

_____ and ate whatever four-legged _____
        NOUN   PLURAL NOUN

he found scurrying around the garbage cans. But now, as ruler of

(the) _____, he is sitting in the _____ of
          A PLACE   NOUN

luxury in a/an _____-shaped palace. His clothes are
                      NOUN

sewed from the finest _____, and he enjoys delicious
                            PLURAL NOUN

four-course _____ three times a day. His throne is
                  PLURAL NOUN

made from solid gold _____, and an enormous
                            PLURAL NOUN

disco _____ hangs in his throne room. All the
            NOUN

prominent residents of the land, such as _____ and
                                              CELEBRITY

_____, flock to his _____ dance parties.
  PERSON IN ROOM   ADJECTIVE

With a snap of the _____, the lights go dim, the
                        PART OF THE BODY (PLURAL)

music grows loud—and witches and _____ guests begin
                                        ADJECTIVE

dancing _____ on the _____ floor! These
              ADVERB   NOUN

days, Rumpel's life is full of fun and _____.
                                            PLURAL NOUN

MAD LIBS® is fun to play with friends, but you can also play it by yourself! To begin with, DO NOT look at the story on the page below. Fill in the blanks on this page with the words called for. Then, using the words you have selected, fill in the blank spaces in the story.

Now you've created your own hilarious MAD LIBS® game!

WANTED: A FEW GOOD WITCHES

ADJECTIVE _____

TYPE OF FOOD _____

ADJECTIVE _____

VERB _____

PLURAL NOUN _____

ADJECTIVE _____

ADJECTIVE _____

PLURAL NOUN _____

PLURAL NOUN _____

VERB ENDING IN "ING" _____

ADJECTIVE _____

NOUN _____

NUMBER _____

PLURAL NOUN _____

PART OF THE BODY _____

PLURAL NOUN _____

VERB _____

MAD LIBS®
WANTED: A FEW GOOD WITCHES

Are you fast and __scary__ on a broom? Can you fire
ADJECTIVE

__monkey brain__ bombs at __slimey__ targets with
TYPE OF FOOD   ADJECTIVE

precision? Do you cackle and __run__ with excitement
VERB

at the thought of capturing smelly, disgusting __black cats__ ?
PLURAL NOUN

If so, then you can become a member of Rumpelstiltskin's

__Haunting__ Witch Patrol. Join our team of __terrifing__
ADJECTIVE   ADJECTIVE

witches who guard His Royal Highness, sweeping the skies with their

__candies__ , and keeping the kingdom free of undesirable
PLURAL NOUN

__broken arms__ ! Although prior experience is not required,
PLURAL NOUN

swooping, diving, and __brain-eating__ abilities on the broom
VERB ENDING IN "ING"

are preferred. Flight gear, including a broom, __gooey__
ADJECTIVE

goggles, and a pointy black __stay puft marshmallow man__, is provided. Starting
NOUN

salary is __1,984__ __spiders__ a week. If you can keep
NUMBER   PLURAL NOUN

your __heart__ to the sky and skillfully dodge such objects
PART OF THE BODY

as birds, planes, and winged __fangs__ , then this job could
PLURAL NOUN

be right for you! __scare__ today for an application!
VERB

MAD LIBS® is fun to play with friends, but you can also play it by yourself! To begin with, DO NOT look at the story on the page below. Fill in the blanks on this page with the words called for. Then, using the words you have selected, fill in the blank spaces in the story.

Now you've created your own hilarious MAD LIBS® game!

NO OGRES ALLOWED

ADJECTIVE _____

ADJECTIVE _____

A PLACE _____

NOUN _____

VERB ENDING IN "ING" _____

ADVERB _____

PART OF THE BODY (PLURAL) _____

A PLACE _____

NUMBER _____

ADJECTIVE _____

ADJECTIVE _____

ADJECTIVE _____

ADJECTIVE _____

VERB ENDING IN "ING" _____

VERB _____

ADJECTIVE _____

MAD LIBS
NO OGRES ALLOWED

Hear ye! Hear ye! By order of His Royal _____-ness,
ADJECTIVE

King Rumpelstiltskin, it is hereby decreed that ogres are

forever banned from the _____ kingdom of (the)
ADJECTIVE

_____. Any of these _____-eating
A PLACE   NOUN

monsters caught _____ on royal lands
VERB ENDING IN "ING"

shall immediately and _____ be bound at the
ADVERB

_____ and carted away to (the) _____.
PART OF THE BODY (PLURAL)   A PLACE

There, they will be sentenced to _____ consecutive
NUMBER

life terms of _____ labor spent making _____
ADJECTIVE   ADJECTIVE

wigs for His _____ Highness. All villagers should
ADJECTIVE

be on the lookout for these gross and _____ creatures.
ADJECTIVE

If you are _____ in the forest and encounter one,
VERB ENDING IN "ING"

run—don't _____!—to the nearest witch precinct to
VERB

report the sighting. When it comes to ogres, it's always better to be

safe than _____!
ADJECTIVE

FROM SHREK FOREVER AFTER MAD LIBS® • Shrek Forever After ™ and © 2010 DreamWorks Animation L.L.C.
Shrek is a registered trademark of DreamWorks Animation L.L.C.All Rights Reserved.
Published by Price Stern Sloan, a division of Penguin Group (USA) Inc., 345 Hudson Street, New York, NY 10014.

MAD LIBS® is fun to play with friends, but you can also play it by yourself! To begin with, DO NOT look at the story on the page below. Fill in the blanks on this page with the words called for. Then, using the words you have selected, fill in the blank spaces in the story.

Now you've created your own hilarious MAD LIBS® game!

BEING DONKEY

CELEBRITY_____

PART OF THE BODY _____

ADJECTIVE _____

NOUN _____

PART OF THE BODY _____

NOUN _____

NOUN _____

PART OF THE BODY (PLURAL) _____

PLURAL NOUN_____

VERB ENDING IN "ING"_____

NUMBER_____

ADJECTIVE _____

NOUN _____

PART OF THE BODY _____

MAD LIBS
BEING DONKEY

Donkey can be as outrageous as _____, but he
CELEBRITY

has a/an _____ of gold! Why do we love this
PART OF THE BODY

_____ donkey? Let's count the ways . . .
ADJECTIVE

1. Born with the gift of _____, this chatty animal
NOUN

can talk your _____ off. He would be a great late
PART OF THE BODY

night talk show _____—except that his guests
NOUN

wouldn't be able to get a/an _____ in edgewise.
NOUN

2. Donkey loves to sing at the top of his _____. His
PART OF THE BODY (PLURAL)

favorite songs are about love and friendship, but he also likes to

croon about _____ and _____ in
PLURAL NOUN   VERB ENDING IN "ING"

the moonlight.

3. The word privacy means nothing to Donkey, who prefers to

be with his friends _____ hours a day. If you
NUMBER

want to spend some _____ time with your
ADJECTIVE

beloved _____, Donkey will be there, sticking his
NOUN

_____ in your business!
PART OF THE BODY

MAD LIBS® is fun to play with friends, but you can also play it by yourself! To begin with, DO NOT look at the story on the page below. Fill in the blanks on this page with the words called for. Then, using the words you have selected, fill in the blank spaces in the story.

Now you've created your own hilarious MAD LIBS® game!

OGRE ARMY

ADJECTIVE _____

PART OF THE BODY _____

PLURAL NOUN _____

ADJECTIVE _____

PERSON IN ROOM _____

ADJECTIVE _____

PLURAL NOUN _____

ADJECTIVE _____

PLURAL NOUN _____

PART OF THE BODY _____

PART OF THE BODY (PLURAL) _____

PLURAL NOUN _____

PLURAL NOUN _____

NOUN _____

PART OF THE BODY _____

ADVERB _____

NOUN _____

MAD LIBS®

OGRE ARMY

Want to join our _____ army of ogres? This life is
ADJECTIVE

not for the faint of _____ ! The best soldiers have
PART OF THE BODY

a deadly combination of brains, brawn, and _____ .
PLURAL NOUN

You must be clever and _____ to plan missions
ADJECTIVE

against the ogres' archenemy, _____ . You'll also
PERSON IN ROOM

spend many _____ hours each day on rigorous
ADJECTIVE

training exercises, fighting against life-sized _____ ,
PLURAL NOUN

and attacking them with _____ axes and battle
ADJECTIVE

_____ . You'll maintain your own gear—a helmet
PLURAL NOUN

to protect your _____ , gauntlets to wear on your
PART OF THE BODY

_____ , and a chest plate formed from cast iron
PART OF THE BODY (PLURAL)

_____ . From cooking _____ over
PLURAL NOUN   PLURAL NOUN

an open campfire to pitching a/an _____ to sleep
NOUN

in, every ogre lends a/an _____ to keep the camp
PART OF THE BODY

running _____ . You may come into the army as an
ADVERB

ogre—but you'll leave as a/an _____ !
NOUN

FROM SHREK FOREVER AFTER MAD LIBS® • Shrek Forever After ™ and © 2010 DreamWorks Animation L.L.C.
Shrek is a registered trademark of DreamWorks Animation L.L.C. All Rights Reserved.
Published by Price Stern Sloan, a division of Penguin Group (USA) Inc., 345 Hudson Street, New York, NY 10014.

MAD LIBS® is fun to play with friends, but you can also play it by yourself! To begin with, DO NOT look at the story on the page below. Fill in the blanks on this page with the words called for. Then, using the words you have selected, fill in the blank spaces in the story.

Now you've created your own hilarious MAD LIBS® game!

HEAD OGRE HEELS

ADJECTIVE _____

ADJECTIVE _____

PLURAL NOUN _____

A PLACE _____

PLURAL NOUN _____

PART OF THE BODY _____

PART OF THE BODY _____

NOUN _____

NOUN _____

ADJECTIVE _____

ADVERB _____

PART OF THE BODY (PLURAL) _____

NOUN _____

VERB _____

PLURAL NOUN _____

MAD LIBS®

HEAD OGRE HEELS

My _____ Fiona,
      ADJECTIVE

I'm not very _____ at expressing myself with words.
           ADJECTIVE

I mean, I'm an ogre—we're not the most romantic _____
                                          PLURAL NOUN

in (the) _____. I thought wooing you with gifts—like a
         A PLACE

heart-shaped box of slimy _____—would make you fall
                        PLURAL NOUN

in love with me. I even made you a coupon book with special offers—

like "One Free _____ Massage." But then I realized this
               PART OF THE BODY

wasn't the way to win your _____. I need to prove to
                      PART OF THE BODY

you that I really know you. So here's what I know, Fiona: I know

that at night, you are an ogre, but by day, you are a beautiful

_____. I know that only true love's _____ will free
    NOUN   NOUN

you from that _____ curse. And I know that if only
                ADJECTIVE

you would look _____ into my _____, you
              ADVERB   PART OF THE BODY (PLURAL)

would see that I'm telling the truth. I am your one true

_____—and I'll love you till the day I _____.
        NOUN   VERB

All my _____, Shrek
       PLURAL NOUN

MAD LIBS® is fun to play with friends, but you can also play it by yourself! To begin with, DO NOT look at the story on the page below. Fill in the blanks on this page with the words called for. Then, using the words you have selected, fill in the blank spaces in the story.

Now you've created your own hilarious MAD LIBS® game!

PAMPERED PUSS

PLURAL NOUN _____

NOUN _____

ADJECTIVE _____

VERB ENDING IN "ING" _____

PART OF THE BODY (PLURAL) _____

PLURAL NOUN _____

PLURAL NOUN _____

PART OF THE BODY _____

ADJECTIVE _____

COLOR _____

NOUN _____

ANIMAL _____

PLURAL NOUN _____

TYPE OF LIQUID _____

NOUN _____

ANIMAL (PLURAL) _____

PART OF THE BODY _____

MAD LIBS®

PAMPERED PUSS

My name was once Puss In _____. Back then, I was a
                          PLURAL NOUN

feared _____ known for my _____
              NOUN   ADJECTIVE

sword-_____. *Dios mio*, I was brilliant. When my
          VERB ENDING IN "ING"

enemies saw me, they'd drop to their _____,
                                           PART OF THE BODY (PLURAL)

begging me to spare their _____. But that was a lifetime
                                PLURAL NOUN

ago. Today I am but a house cat—a tent cat, actually—the beloved

pet of Fiona, the tough-as-_____ leader of the ogre
                                 PLURAL NOUN

army. Is it an easier life? *Sí*, I will admit it is. These days, I just sit

around and lick my _____. My fur is so soft from
                          PART OF THE BODY

_____ brushing. I traded in my boots and sword for
     ADJECTIVE

a frilly _____ _____. I take _____ naps
            COLOR   NOUN   ANIMAL

on pillows filled with the softest _____. I have all the
                                        PLURAL NOUN

_____ I could ever want, and it's served to me on a
     TYPE OF LIQUID

silver-plated _____ engraved with my name. And I
                      NOUN

could have all the _____ to snack on, too—if I could
                        ANIMAL (PLURAL)

just get off my supersized _____ to catch them.
                                  PART OF THE BODY

MAD LIBS® is fun to play with friends, but you can also play it by yourself! To begin with, DO NOT look at the story on the page below. Fill in the blanks on this page with the words called for. Then, using the words you have selected, fill in the blank spaces in the story.

Now you've created your own hilarious MAD LIBS® game!

RUMPEL WIGS OUT

VERB _____

ADJECTIVE _____

PERSON IN ROOM (MALE) _____

NOUN _____

NOUN _____

NUMBER_____

PLURAL NOUN_____

PART OF THE BODY _____

VERB _____

COLOR _____

NOUN _____

NOUN _____

MAD LIBS
RUMPEL WIGS OUT

Beware the hair! When Rumpelstiltskin puts on one of his wigs,

it's best to _____ for cover! No good can come from
VERB

this, as many of the _____ townsfolk of Far Far Away
ADJECTIVE

discovered. For example, one time, when Rumpel was wearing his

confused wig, _____ asked to be transformed from a
PERSON IN ROOM (MALE)

wooden _____ into a real boy—but Rumpel changed
NOUN

him into a/an _____ instead! Another time, Rumpel
NOUN

was wearing his angry wig when the _____ Pigs wanted
NUMBER

him to give them an invincible house made of _____.
PLURAL NOUN

You could practically see the steam coming out of his

_____ as he ordered Wolfie to huff and puff and
PART OF THE BODY

_____ their house down instead! And everybody knows
VERB

to steer clear whenever Rumpel wears his _____ joker
COLOR

wig. Once, Gingy asked Rumpel to help him run, run as fast as a/an

_____—so Rumpel sent a hungry _____ after
NOUN   NOUN

him. It made Gingy run, all right!

MAD LIBS® is fun to play with friends, but you can also play it by yourself! To begin with, DO NOT look at the story on the page below. Fill in the blanks on this page with the words called for. Then, using the words you have selected, fill in the blank spaces in the story.

Now you've created your own hilarious MAD LIBS® game!

FIONA FIRES UP HER ARMY

NOUN _____

PART OF THE BODY _____

VERB (PAST TENSE) _____

TYPE OF LIQUID_____

PLURAL NOUN_____

NOUN _____

NOUN _____

PERSON IN ROOM _____

NOUN _____

TYPE OF FOOD _____

PLURAL NOUN_____

A PLACE_____

ADJECTIVE _____

ADJECTIVE _____

MAD LIBS®
FIONA FIRES UP HER ARMY

My fellow ogres, as we stand together as a united _____ ,
NOUN

I confess that my _____ is pounding with excitement.
PART OF THE BODY

We have _____ long and hard to get to where we
VERB (PAST TENSE)

are. All the blood, sweat, and _____ we poured
TYPE OF LIQUID

into perfecting our combat techniques have prepared us well.

Rumpelstiltskin and his band of evil _____ will be no
PLURAL NOUN

match for us! Brogan, my right-hand _____ , your valor
NOUN

and intelligence have helped make me a better _____ .
NOUN

Private _____ , your hard work and enthusiasm show
PERSON IN ROOM

me that you will someday be a great _____ . And
NOUN

Cookie, your loyalty to this resistance is as firm and unyielding

as your roasted _____ . Now let's rise up and fight
TYPE OF FOOD

like _____ to take down Rumpelstiltskin and restore
PLURAL NOUN

peace to (the) _____ . Our battle will be hard fought,
A PLACE

but victory will be _____ ! Get out there, and make
ADJECTIVE

me—and all ogres—very _____ !
ADJECTIVE

FROM SHREK FOREVER AFTER MAD LIBS® • Shrek Forever After ™ and © 2010 DreamWorks Animation L.L.C.
Shrek is a registered trademark of DreamWorks Animation L.L.C. All Rights Reserved.
Published by Price Stern Sloan, a division of Penguin Group (USA) Inc., 345 Hudson Street, New York, NY 10014.

MAD LIBS® is fun to play with friends, but you can also play it by yourself! To begin with, DO NOT look at the story on the page below. Fill in the blanks on this page with the words called for. Then, using the words you have selected, fill in the blank spaces in the story.

Now you've created your own hilarious MAD LIBS® game!

PAY THE PIPER

ADJECTIVE _____

PLURAL NOUN _____

NOUN _____

ADJECTIVE _____

ADJECTIVE _____

VERB _____

ADJECTIVE _____

NOUN _____

ADJECTIVE _____

NOUN _____

ADJECTIVE _____

SAME ADJECTIVE _____

A PLACE _____

CELEBRITY _____

PERSON IN ROOM _____

PERSON IN ROOM _____

A PLACE _____

PART OF THE BODY _____

PLURAL NOUN _____

MAD LIBS®
PAY THE PIPER

Overrun with _____ rodents? Infested with _____?
              ADJECTIVE   PLURAL NOUN

Fear not! Help is just a/an _____ away! The Pied
                                       NOUN

Piper will help you clean house! He uses a top-of-the-line,

_____ flute to blow away your pesky problems.
ADJECTIVE

Are _____ ogres taking over? He'll set his flute to
          ADJECTIVE

"_____" and play a/an _____
         VERB   ADJECTIVE

tune to lead them away. It's easy as _____ ! No pest
                                     NOUN

is too _____ for this great _____ to
     ADJECTIVE   NOUN

conquer. The Pied Piper's reputation is known far and wide—

from the kingdom of _____ _____
                  ADJECTIVE   SAME ADJECTIVE

Away across the seas to the land of (the) _____ .
                                          A PLACE

He counts _____ and _____
               CELEBRITY   PERSON IN ROOM

as satisfied, repeat customers! _____ from
                             PERSON IN ROOM

(the) _____ says, "The Pied Piper really
             A PLACE

kicks _____!" So, call today—and kiss your
     PART OF THE BODY

_____ good-bye!
PLURAL NOUN

MAD LIBS® is fun to play with friends, but you can also play it by yourself! To begin with, DO NOT look at the story on the page below. Fill in the blanks on this page with the words called for. Then, using the words you have selected, fill in the blank spaces in the story.

Now you've created your own hilarious MAD LIBS® game!

THE GREAT ESCAPE

PLURAL NOUN _____

NUMBER _____

ADJECTIVE _____

VERB ENDING IN "ING" _____

PART OF THE BODY (PLURAL) _____

PLURAL NOUN _____

PLURAL NOUN _____

NOUN _____

PART OF THE BODY (PLURAL) _____

NOUN _____

PART OF THE BODY _____

PART OF THE BODY _____

PLURAL NOUN _____

ADJECTIVE _____

NOUN _____

MAD LIBS®

THE GREAT ESCAPE

Fiona looked at all the _____ she had carved
                               PLURAL NOUN

into the wall of the tower where she had been held prisoner

for _____ years. She had been locked in this
          NUMBER

_____ cell for what seemed like an eternity. With Prince
   ADJECTIVE

_____ nowhere in sight, she took matters into her
   VERB ENDING IN "ING"

own _____ and rescued herself! While the dragon
      PART OF THE BODY (PLURAL)

who guarded the castle was busy hunting _____ ,
                                              PLURAL NOUN

she threw _____ at it. The dragon came charging
              PLURAL NOUN

like a/an _____ at Fiona. She raced to the castle
              NOUN

entrance, the dragon hot on her _____ . But a
                                     PART OF THE BODY (PLURAL)

giant _____ was blocking the doorway! Fiona
          NOUN

dived _____ -first under the door. The dragon was
          PART OF THE BODY

too big and slammed her _____ right into it! The
                             PART OF THE BODY

dragon fired flaming _____ at Fiona, but she was too
                          PLURAL NOUN

_____ . She had escaped by a/an _____!
   ADJECTIVE   NOUN

At last, Fiona was free!

MAD LIBS® is fun to play with friends, but you can also play it by yourself! To begin with, DO NOT look at the story on the page below. Fill in the blanks on this page with the words called for. Then, using the words you have selected, fill in the blank spaces in the story.

Now you've created your own hilarious MAD LIBS® game!

AN UN-CHANTING LIFE

PERSON IN ROOM (MALE) _____

PERSON IN ROOM (FEMALE) _____

ADJECTIVE _____

ADJECTIVE _____

NOUN _____

PLURAL NOUN _____

NOUN _____

NOUN _____

PLURAL NOUN _____

PART OF THE BODY _____

ANIMAL _____

PLURAL NOUN _____

PLURAL NOUN _____

PART OF THE BODY (PLURAL) _____

ADJECTIVE _____

MAD LIBS®
AN UN-CHANTING LIFE

Under the kind and just rule of King _____ and
<u>PERSON IN ROOM (MALE)</u>

Queen _____, the land of Far Far Away was safe,
<u>PERSON IN ROOM (FEMALE)</u>

prosperous, and _____. But when Rumpelstiltskin
<u>ADJECTIVE</u>

became king, life took a turn for the _____!
<u>ADJECTIVE</u>

Donkey had to pull a/an _____ containing captured
<u>NOUN</u>

_____ . The Muffin Man's _____
<u>PLURAL NOUN</u>   <u>NOUN</u>

business was forced to close down, so to make enough dough

to pay the bills, he and Gingy ran a/an _____-fighting
<u>NOUN</u>

operation. The Three Little _____ were enslaved
<u>PLURAL NOUN</u>

by Rumpel and forced to wait hand and _____ on
<u>PART OF THE BODY</u>

him and his pet _____ , Fifi. Wolfie was forced to
<u>ANIMAL</u>

clean and maintain all the _____ that Rumpel wore
<u>PLURAL NOUN</u>

on his head. The loyal _____ of Far Far Away could
<u>PLURAL NOUN</u>

only cross their _____ in hope that someday,
<u>PART OF THE BODY (PLURAL)</u>

someone would come to their rescue and return Far Far Away to the

_____ kingdom it once was.
<u>ADJECTIVE</u>

MAD LIBS® is fun to play with friends, but you can also play it by yourself! To begin with, DO NOT look at the story on the page below. Fill in the blanks on this page with the words called for. Then, using the words you have selected, fill in the blank spaces in the story.

Now you've created your own hilarious MAD LIBS® game!

DINNER AND A SHOW

ADJECTIVE _____

PART OF THE BODY _____

TYPE OF LIQUID_____

PLURAL NOUN_____

ADJECTIVE _____

ADJECTIVE _____

PLURAL NOUN_____

ANIMAL_____

ADJECTIVE _____

ADJECTIVE _____

PART OF THE BODY (PLURAL) _____

VERB _____

PART OF THE BODY (PLURAL) _____

ADVERB _____

MAD LIBS®

DINNER AND A SHOW

Cookie, the ogre army's chef, has a/an _____ life

ADJECTIVE

motto: Never go into battle on an empty _____.

PART OF THE BODY

On the eve of the uprising against Rumpelstiltskin, Cookie made a

steaming pot of hearty eyeball _____ and served it

TYPE OF LIQUID

with fresh _____ and butter! He also whipped up

PLURAL NOUN

some _____ dishes using only the finest ingredients—

ADJECTIVE

aged mud, _____ slugs, rotten _____,

ADJECTIVE   PLURAL NOUN

and more eyeballs. The ogres love to chomp on those eyeballs,

especially _____ eyeballs, since those are extra

ANIMAL

_____ . When the ogres finished their pre-battle meal,

ADJECTIVE

they all let out _____ burps! But the meal wouldn't be

ADJECTIVE

complete without entertainment. Donkey stuck some eyeballs in

his _____ and made the ogres _____

PART OF THE BODY (PLURAL)   VERB

so hard, soup came squirting out of their _____!

PART OF THE BODY (PLURAL)

Now that they were well fed and _____ entertained,

ADVERB

the ogres were ready for battle!

MAD LIBS® is fun to play with friends, but you can also play it by yourself! To begin with, DO NOT look at the story on the page below. Fill in the blanks on this page with the words called for. Then, using the words you have selected, fill in the blank spaces in the story.

Now you've created your own hilarious MAD LIBS® game!

ONE TOUGH COOKIE

PART OF THE BODY (PLURAL) _____

NOUN _____

NOUN _____

PART OF THE BODY (PLURAL) _____

PLURAL NOUN_____

VERB _____

PART OF THE BODY (PLURAL) _____

ADJECTIVE _____

TYPE OF LIQUID_____

ADJECTIVE _____

NOUN _____

NOUN _____

VERB _____

SAME VERB _____

NOUN _____

MAD LIBS
ONE TOUGH COOKIE

"Drop to your _____ and give me twenty!"
PART OF THE BODY (PLURAL)

Gingy snapped at his cookies-in-training. Yes, this gladiator

had once been a soft-hearted _____, but these days he
NOUN

was one tough _____ ! To firm up his recruits' doughy
NOUN

_____ , Gingy made them lift _____
PART OF THE BODY (PLURAL)   PLURAL NOUN

and do a series of crunches and _____-ups. To keep
VERB

them light on their _____ , Gingy timed them while
PART OF THE BODY (PLURAL)

they ran _____ laps around the kitchen. He worked
ADJECTIVE

them until they were dripping with _____ ! But
TYPE OF LIQUID

a good warrior has a strong body and a/an _____
ADJECTIVE

mind. So Gingy made his trainees look in the mirror and snarl,

"Are you a man—or a/an _____? Go ahead, punk—
NOUN

make my _____ !" Gingy taught the cookies that, as
NOUN

warriors, you can't _____ with the enemy, but you
VERB

can't _____ without them, either. That's just the way
SAME VERB

the _____ crumbles!
NOUN

MAD LIBS® is fun to play with friends, but you can also play it by yourself! To begin with, DO NOT look at the story on the page below. Fill in the blanks on this page with the words called for. Then, using the words you have selected, fill in the blank spaces in the story.

Now you've created your own hilarious MAD LIBS® game!

BREAKING NEWS FROM THE CASTLE

PERSON IN ROOM _____

NUMBER_____

ADJECTIVE _____

ADJECTIVE _____

ADJECTIVE _____

PERSON IN ROOM (MALE) _____

NOUN _____

NOUN _____

ADJECTIVE _____

NOUN _____

EXCLAMATION _____

ADJECTIVE _____

PART OF THE BODY (PLURAL) _____

PERSON IN ROOM _____

ADJECTIVE _____

MAD LIBS
BREAKING NEWS
FROM THE CASTLE

This is _____ "Scoop" Newman of WFAR-Channel
_____ PERSON IN ROOM

_____ with a/an _____ news update. I'm live on the
NUMBER   ADJECTIVE

scene in Rumpelstiltskin's throne room where a/an _____
                 ADJECTIVE

battle is taking place. Here's what we know: Led by the brave

and _____ Donkey and _____ In Boots,
    ADJECTIVE   PERSON IN ROOM (MALE)

the ogre army busted into Rumpel's _____ to overthrow
                         NOUN

him and save Shrek and Fiona. At this very moment, the

twosome is chained in a dungeon with a fire-breathing

_____. Up above, ogres and witches are pounding
NOUN

one another with _____ bombs and _____
            ADJECTIVE   NOUN

chimichangas. _____, now Puss and Donkey have
         EXCLAMATION

fallen into the dungeon! Things are not looking _____
                      ADJECTIVE

for our heroes. If they manage to get out of this mess, it'll

be by the skin of their _____ ! Let's check the
          PART OF THE BODY (PLURAL)

weather with the lovely _____ , and we'll be right back
           PERSON IN ROOM

with more updates as this _____ battle unfolds!
           ADJECTIVE

MAD LIBS® is fun to play with friends, but you can also play it by yourself! To begin with, DO NOT look at the story on the page below. Fill in the blanks on this page with the words called for. Then, using the words you have selected, fill in the blank spaces in the story.

Now you've created your own hilarious MAD LIBS® game!

HOW TO FLY A BROOM, BY DONKEY

ADJECTIVE _____

ADJECTIVE _____

NOUN _____

PART OF THE BODY (PLURAL) _____

PLURAL NOUN _____

VERB _____

PERSON IN ROOM _____

NOUN _____

PLURAL NOUN _____

PLURAL NOUN _____

NOUN _____

ADJECTIVE _____

PART OF THE BODY _____

SILLY WORD _____

MAD LIBS®
HOW TO FLY A BROOM, BY DONKEY

Hey, it's me, Donkey. Since I've spent so much time with Rumpel's

_____ witches, I thought I'd share some _____
<u>ADJECTIVE</u>   <u>ADJECTIVE</u>

flying tips I've learned. Who says you have to be a wicked old

_____ to fly a broom? All you need to know is this:
<u>NOUN</u>

1. Never put your hooves over the _____ of the
                       <u>PART OF THE BODY (PLURAL)</u>

   person driving, or scream, "Oh, my _____, we're going
                              <u>PLURAL NOUN</u>

   to _____!" (I did that to _____ on my first
        <u>VERB</u>   <u>PERSON IN ROOM</u>

   flight, and we almost crashed into a/an _____!)
                                     <u>NOUN</u>

2. Don't bring along any carry-on _____. There's no room
                               <u>PLURAL NOUN</u>

   for them!

3. Brooms work best when ridden solo. If you need to travel with

   two or more _____, I recommend traveling by a/an
                  <u>PLURAL NOUN</u>

   _____-drawn carriage instead.
     <u>NOUN</u>

4. Controlling a/an _____ broom can be tricky because
                     <u>ADJECTIVE</u>

   sometimes it has a/an _____ of its own. So when
                     <u>PART OF THE BODY</u>

   you want to stop, just yank the tip and yell, "_____!"
                                      <u>SILLY WORD</u>

   (And if that doesn't work, try yelling "Mommy!")

MAD LIBS® is fun to play with friends, but you can also play it by yourself! To begin with, DO NOT look at the story on the page below. Fill in the blanks on this page with the words called for. Then, using the words you have selected, fill in the blank spaces in the story.

Now you've created your own hilarious MAD LIBS® game!

RUMPEL IS RUINED!

ADJECTIVE _____

PLURAL NOUN _____

PLURAL NOUN _____

NOUN _____

A PLACE _____

NOUN _____

PERSON IN ROOM _____

NOUN _____

NUMBER _____

PLURAL NOUN _____

ADJECTIVE _____

NOUN _____

ADJECTIVE _____

NOUN _____

PLURAL NOUN _____

NOUN _____

PLURAL NOUN _____

MAD LIBS

RUMPEL IS RUINED!

Poor Rumpel! Conquered by the _____ army of
ADJECTIVE

_____ , his reign of _____ was over.
PLURAL NOUN   PLURAL NOUN

He had lost his crown, his kingdom, and his _____!
NOUN

Banished forever from (the) _____ , Rumpel
A PLACE

and his pet _____ , _____ , were
NOUN   PERSON IN ROOM

forced to go from living in the _____ of luxury
NOUN

to living like paupers. Instead of three _____-course
NUMBER

meals a day, they had to rummage through garbage cans for scraps

of moldy _____ to eat. Instead of a nice, warm bed
PLURAL NOUN

with _____ sheets, Rumpel was forced to sleep
ADJECTIVE

under a/an _____ in the dark, _____
NOUN   ADJECTIVE

forest. And no more fine clothes, either! Alas, he had nothing

but the tattered _____ on his back and ragged
NOUN

_____ on his feet. Now, instead of being a pampered
PLURAL NOUN

royal _____ , Rumpel has to clean witches'
NOUN

_____ to make a living!
PLURAL NOUN

FROM SHREK FOREVER AFTER MAD LIBS® • Shrek Forever After ™ and © 2010 DreamWorks Animation L.L.C.
Shrek is a registered trademark of DreamWorks Animation L.L.C.All Rights Reserved.
Published by Price Stern Sloan, a division of Penguin Group (USA) Inc., 345 Hudson Street, New York, NY 10014.

MAD LIBS® is fun to play with friends, but you can also play it by yourself! To begin with, DO NOT look at the story on the page below. Fill in the blanks on this page with the words called for. Then, using the words you have selected, fill in the blank spaces in the story.

Now you've created your own hilarious MAD LIBS® game!

HAPPY FOREVER AFTER

ADJECTIVE _____

PLURAL NOUN _____

ADJECTIVE _____

PART OF THE BODY _____

NOUN _____

PLURAL NOUN _____

ADJECTIVE _____

NOUN _____

ADJECTIVE _____

PERSON IN ROOM _____

ADJECTIVE _____

ADJECTIVE _____

PART OF THE BODY _____

PLURAL NOUN _____

VERB (PAST TENSE) _____

MAD LIBS®

HAPPY FOREVER AFTER

After almost losing everything he loved, Shrek realized how

_____ he really had it. He began to count all the
ADJECTIVE

_____ in his life, including:
PLURAL NOUN

• a doting, _____ wife who loved him with all
ADJECTIVE

her _____ and made him feel like the best
PART OF THE BODY

_____ in the world
NOUN

• three adorable _____ who thought their
PLURAL NOUN

_____ daddy was the greatest thing since
ADJECTIVE

roasted _____ rats
NOUN

• _____ friends like Donkey, Puss, and _____,
ADJECTIVE   PERSON IN ROOM

who stuck by him through thick and _____
ADJECTIVE

• _____ days filled with mud baths,
ADJECTIVE

_____-tinis, and lots of love, laughter, and
PART OF THE BODY

_____
PLURAL NOUN

So in the end, Shrek, his family, and friends all _____
VERB (PAST TENSE)

happily ever after!

This book is published by

PSS!
PRICE STERN SLOAN

whose other splendid titles include
such literary classics as